To Uncle Mike – for stories and songs.
To Arthur – who carries them on – SPC

For my dear family and friends. Your support and cheer
mean the world to me, I love you all to the moon and back.
A special thank you to Janetta and Judith for their vision
and patient guidance throughout – RS

About the Story

The King with Dirty Feet is inspired by an Indian folktale called *The King and the Cobbler*, which is included in *The Thief of Love: Bengali Tales from Court and Village*, edited by Edward C Dimock, University of Chicago Press, 1963.
The King with Dirty Feet by Sally Pomme Clayton was originally published in *Time for Telling*, edited by Mary Medlicott and illustrated by Sue Williams, Kingfisher, 1991.

Text copyright © Sally Pomme Clayton 1991, 2018
Illustrations copyright © Rhiannon Sanderson 2018
First published in Great Britain and in the USA in 2018 by
Otter-Barry Books, Little Orchard, Burley Gate, Hereford, HR1 3QS
www.otterbarrybooks.com

A catalogue record for this book is available from the British Library.

ISBN 978-1-91095-923-7

Illustrated with mixed media and photoshop

Printed in China

1 3 5 7 9 8 6 4 2

The King
with
Dirty Feet

Written by **Sally Pomme Clayton**

Illustrated by **Rhiannon Sanderson**

Once upon a time there was a king.
He lived in a beautiful palace in India.

His kingdom was filled with trees,
flowers, animals, and a lovely river.
The king had everything he wanted
and was very happy.

But there was one thing that this king hated,
and that was bathtime.

The king had not washed for a week,
he had not washed for a month,
he had not washed for a whole year!
And he had begun to smell.

He smelt underneath his arms, in between
his toes, behind his ears and up his nose.
He was the smelliest king there has even been.

His servant Gabu was very polite about the smell.
But nobody liked to be near the king.

Then, one day, the smell became too much
for the king himself!
And the king said, rather sadly,
"I think it is time I had a bath."

The king walked slowly down
to the river. But news
travelled fast.

"The king's going to have a bath!"

Everyone rushed down to
the river bank to get the best view.

They all fell silent, as the king stepped
into the cool, clear river water.
When the king called for the Royal Soap,
a huge cheer arose.

The king washed and scrubbed
and brushed his teeth.
He played with his toy ducks
and little boat.

Then, at last, when he was quite clean,
he called for the Royal Towel and
stepped out of the river.

When the king had finished drying himself,
he looked at his feet, and they were
covered with dust.

"I forgot to wash them!" he said.

The king stepped back into the water.
He rubbed his feet with bubbles of soap.
Then he stepped out of the river,
but his feet were

STILL DIRTY!

"I didn't wash them enough," he said crossly.
"Bring me the Royal Scrubbing Brush."

The king scrubbed his feet until they shone.
But as soon as he stepped on dry land,
his feet were DIRTY again.

The king was furious. He called for his servant.
Gabu came running, and bowed low.

"Gabu," boomed the king. "The king has had a bath.
The king is clean. But the land is dirty. There is dust
everywhere. Get rid of all this dirt, so my feet stay clean."

"Yes, Your Majesty," replied Gabu.

"You have three days to rid the land of dirt,
and if you fail, do you know what will
happen to you?" asked the king.

"No, Your Majesty."

"**ZUT!**" cried the king.

"**ZUT!**" said Gabu. "What is **ZUT**?"

"**ZUT!** is the sound of your head being chopped off."

Gabu began to cry.

"Don't waste time, Gabu," said the king.
"Rid the land of dirt at once."

"I must put my thinking cap on," said Gabu.
He put his head in his hands and thought.
"When something is dirty, you... brush it!"

Gabu asked everyone to help him.
People took brushes and brooms and...

ONE... TWO... THREE...

they all began to sweep – swish, swish, swish, swish –
all day long.

Dust filled the air in a thick, dark cloud.
Everyone started coughing and spluttering
and bumping into each other.

The king choked, "Gabu, where are you?
I asked you to rid the land of dust,
not fill the air with dust. You have two
more days, or

ZUT!"

"Oh dear, oh dear," cried Gabu, and he put his head in his hands and thought.

"When something is dirty, you... wash it!"

Gabu asked everyone to help him. They took buckets and pails, filled them with water and...

ONE... TWO... THREE...
they all began to pour – sloosh, sloosh, sloosh, sloosh – all day long. Water spread across the land and began to rise. Water reached everyone's ankles, rose up to their knees, up to their waists, and reached their chins.

"Swim, everybody!" cried Gabu.

The king climbed to the top of the highest mountain.
Water lapped his toes, and he sniffed,

"Gabu, a...atchoo! Where are you?"

Gabu came swimming.

"Yes, Your Majesty?"

"Gabu, I asked you to rid the land of dirt,
not turn the kingdom into a swimming pool.
You have one more day, or

ZUT!"

"Oh dear, oh dear, I've run out of ideas," cried Gabu.
He put his head in his hands and thought
and thought.

"When something is dirty, you... cover it up!"

Gabu asked everyone to help him.
They took needles and threads and pieces of cloth,
and...

ONE... TWO... THREE...
they all began to sew –
stitch, stitch, stitch, stitch –
all day long.

The cloth got **bigger** and **bigger**. They stitched all the pieces of cloth together, into one huge cloth that spread across the land.

It fitted perfectly. It stretched from the school to the well, from the temple to the palace, and all the way down to the river.

"We've done it!" cried Gabu.
"We're ready, Your Majesty!"

The king peeped out of the palace.
The ground looked clean –
very clean indeed.
The king put one foot on the cloth,
and there was not a speck of dust.

"Comfortable and clean," said the king.
"The dirt has gone! Well done, Gabu."

Then a little old man with a long white beard
stepped out of the crowd. He bowed low before the king.

"Your Majesty, how will anything grow, now that
the land is covered with cloth? There will be no grass
or flowers. The animals will be hungry.
There will be no fruit or vegetables to eat."

"We need dirt so that we can live," said the old man.
"Your Majesty, you don't have to
cover the land with cloth
to keep your feet clean."

The old man took a pair of scissors
out of his pocket. He bent down
and began to cut the cloth
around the king's feet –
snip, snip, snip, snip.

He cut out two small pieces of cloth.

Then the old man took two long laces,
and tied the pieces of cloth to the king's feet.

"Try them, Your Majesty."

The king looked down at his feet.
He had never seen anything like it.
He put one foot forward.

"Very good," he exclaimed. He took a step.
"Splendid." The king walked.
"Comfortable, clean, and the grass can grow!"

The king ran and jumped.

"Hooray," he cried. "I can walk here,
and here, and here. I can walk anywhere
and my feet will always be clean!"

What was the king wearing on his feet?
He was wearing **SHOES!**
They were the first pair of shoes
ever made,

and people have been wearing shoes ever since.